A SEEK AND SOLVE MYSTERY!

Monsters on the Loose!

By Bruce Hale
Illustrations by
Dave Garbot

HARPER
An Imprint of HarperCollinsPublishers

The Suspects...

All the monsters are in a muddle. Someone stole every last bit of candy, and it's almost Halloween! Frankenstein's Monster is hot on the case—can you help him figure out who did it?

Vampire Bob

Joey Bones

Igor

Willy the Werewolf

Find the clues hidden on each page and help Frankie catch the candy thief. But you'd better be quick about it— Halloween is coming. Time is running out!

Rowan the Witch

Nefertiti

Frankie has just spotted something that the candy-napper left behind. Here's your first clue—find Frankenstein's Monster, and see what he's holding.

Bobo's Bat Nook is dark and spooky. It's hard to find clues, but not for Frankie. He's tracked down something suspicious. Do you see what it is?

Henry's Haunted House is hopping with excitement, but it looks like the robber's been here, too. Find the Big Green Guy, and see what he's discovered.

As Frankie searches Creepy Acres, he notices something the thief must have dropped. Where's Frankie, and what's he holding?

At Farmer Fang's Pumpkin
Patch, Frankie sniffs out another clue.
But where, oh where in the fields can he be?

Everyone's all aquiver at Sylvester's Spooky Park, and it's not from the thrill rides. Could Frankenstein's Monster have found a trace of the candy thief?

Out on the Misty Moors, the werewolves are all worked up. The robber left something behind when he passed this way. Spot Frankie, and see what it is.

Getting into the spirit of things, Frankenstein's Monster drops by the Ghost Grotto. Time is running short, but he's found another clue. Now, can *you* find *Frankie*?

Tarantula Town is crawling with news—the thief has been here, too! Locate Frankie, and see what he's spotted.

While getting lost in the case, Ol' Bolts-in-the-Neck discovers something odd in the maze. Now if he can only find his way out!

Back home at Dr. Frankenstein's castle, Frankie stumbles onto one last clue, and it's a doozy. Find him, and see if you can wrap up the case.

So . . . have you figured out who took all the Halloween candy? Let's look at the clues again.

The Evidence . . .

Eye Patch

Black Ribbon

Candy Apple

Pirate Hat

Pocket Watch

**Black
Bow Tie**

**Candy
Corn**

**Trick or Treat
Bag**

**Broomstick
Straw**

**Torn
Candy
Wrapper**

Flashlight

That's right! It was Igor!

He collected the candy for a monster-sized Halloween party at the castle. Igor sure looks pleased with himself. But Frankie's not smiling—maybe some candy will cheer him up?